Ill
Will,
Well
Nell

If you enjoy reading this book, you might
also like to try another story
from the MAMMOTH STORYBOOK series:

Ill Will,  Well Nell

Jenny Nimmo

Illustrated by David Wyn Millward

Mammoth

For Guilsfield Primary School, where I met Will.
J.N.

First published in Great Britain in 2000 by Mammoth
an imprint of Egmont Children's Books Limited,
239 Kensington High Street, London W8 6SA

Text copyright © 2000 Jenny Nimmo
Illustrations copyright © 2000 David Wynn Millward
Cover illustration copyright © 2000 Lynne Chapman

The moral rights of the author, illustrator and cover
illustrator have been asserted.

The rights of Jenny Nimmo, David Wynn Millward and
Lynne Chapman to be identified as the author, illustrator and
cover illustrator of this work have been asserted by them in
accordance with the Copyright, Designs and Patents Act 1988

ISBN 0 7497 3910 X

10 9 8 7 6 5 4 3 2

A CIP catalogue record for this title
is available from the British Library

Printed in Great Britain
by Cox & Wyman Ltd, Reading Berkshire

Contents

~

1. The almost-tree-house

Will and Nell Shepherd lived on a farm. Their house was built on the side of a hill and from every window they could see fields and sheep and sky.

Things happened to Will: accidents, illnesses, sick-bugs, coughs, earaches and all sorts of nasty things.

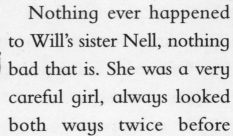

Nothing ever happened to Will's sister Nell, nothing bad that is. She was a very careful girl, always looked both ways twice before crossing the road, always wore her luminous strap and safety helmet when she was bicycling after tea, always wore her hood up on rainy days, washed her hands before meals and put sun-cream on her nose if it was very sunny.

As Will did none of these things you can imagine the sort of trouble he got into. Will didn't *enjoy* being ill. He didn't *try* to get ill. He just forgot to be careful. For instance, there was the tree-house accident.

Will had always wanted a tree-house and his dad said he could have one for his birthday. Mr Shepherd chose a big sycamore tree quite close to the house. 'We can keep an eye on you there,' he told Will.

'And I can keep an eye on you,' said Will.

'Can I go in the tree-house?' asked Nell.

'Of course,' said Mr Shepherd.

'Of course *not*,' said Will. 'It's my tree-house, and you're too young. You'd do something silly.'

'I'm very careful,' Nell pointed out.

'Nell won't do any harm, I'm sure,' added Mr Shepherd.

'She's too small,' whined Will. 'She'd fall out. And, anyway, it's my birthday present, isn't it?'

Mr Shepherd shrugged and muttered, 'Yes, but presents can be shared.'

Next day, when Will and Nell came home from school, there was a rope ladder hanging from the sycamore tree. And over two wide branches that ran out from the trunk, a wide platform had been built.

'The floor of my tree-house!' Will shouted. 'Yippee!' He climbed up the ladder and began to bounce on the wooden platform.

Nell looked up at the almost-tree-house. She imagined having tea up there, with her friend Fiona. Everything would taste good in a tree-house, Nell thought, even custard which she usually hated.

'Come down, Will!' called Mr Shepherd.
'Those planks haven't been nailed in
properly, yet. Besides, Mum says it's tea-
time.'

Will climbed down the ladder which
swayed as he moved. Nell watched and
thought, I could do that, easy as pie.

That night it rained. The wind howled
and lightning flashed across the sky. It rained
all the next day as well. When Will and Nell
came home from school, the tree-house

hadn't been built. All the planks were still neatly stacked in the garage.

Will asked why nothing had been done and his dad said, 'Look at the rain. I can't build a tree-house in weather like this.'

'Is it going to be ready tomorrow?' Will asked.

'It depends on the weather,' said Mr Shepherd.

'But my birthday's on Saturday,' Will moaned. 'Only two days left. What am I going to tell Sam and Daniel and Wayne and . . . and Brian and Mike and Josh and Ben and Tim . . . and . . . and . . . the twins and . . .'

'Goodness,' said Mrs Shepherd. 'How many boys are coming?'

'Twelve,' said Will. 'And . . .'

'Hold on, Will, you'll never get twelve boys in the tree-house all at once,' said Mr Shepherd.

'We'll take it in turns,' said Will.

Nell thought, two girls would fit in a tree-house very nicely. If there is a tree-house.

It rained again in the night, and all the next day. When Will and Nell came home from school, Mr Shepherd looked rather solemn.

'I'm sorry, Will,' he said. 'I didn't have a chance to fix your tree-house. It's been too wet.'

'Only one day left!' cried Will. 'You promised me a tree-house for my birthday.'

Mrs Shepherd tried to change the subject. 'There's a present for you, Will.' She handed

him a small package.
'It's from Gran.'

'Can I open it, now?'
asked Will.

'Save it for Saturday,'
said his mum. 'And
don't look so glum,
Will. You can still have
a party. Just tell your friends to come again
when the tree-house is ready.'

'It's not the same,' Will grumbled. He
didn't say a word at tea-time, he didn't even
smile at Mr Shepherd's jokes.

After tea Mr Shepherd went to a meeting
in the village. Will stomped off to watch TV
in the sitting-room. Nell followed. After a
few moments Will began to cheer up. Nell
could tell that he'd had an idea. She could
almost see it making its way across Will's
face. Suddenly he jumped up and rubbed his
hands together. 'Yes,' he murmured.

'Yes, what?' said Nell.

'I'm going out for a bit,' Will told her.

'But it's raining, you'll get wet.'

'So I'll put on my anorak and wellies.'

'Where are you going?'

Will was just about to tell Nell to mind her own business when he thought better of it. Nell might help him if he was nice to her.

'I'm going to finish the tree-house myself,' he whispered.

Nell gasped. 'You can't, you'll fall,' she whispered back.

'No I won't. You just keep Mum busy and don't you dare tell her where I am or what I'm doing. Promise?'

'Promise,' said Nell, very reluctantly. 'But be careful.'

From the window she watched her

brother running across the garden. He hadn't put his hood up and the rain was coming down in bucketfuls.

Nell shook her head, then she went to help her mum in the kitchen. Mrs Shepherd had made a big chocolate cake for Will's birthday. 'You can decorate it,' she told Nell.

Nell began to edge the cake with coloured icing. It was warm and peaceful in the kitchen, you couldn't hear the rain at all. After a while her mum said, 'It's very quiet. Where's Will?'

Nell didn't know what to say. She hated telling lies. It always made her feel hot and uncomfortable. But she'd made a promise to Will and she couldn't break it.

'He's in his room,' she said at last.

Soon it got so dark in the kitchen, Mum had to switch the light on. Thunder rolled across the hills and the wind started to howl.

Nell began to feel a little nagging pain in

the pit of her stomach. She wondered what had happened to Will.

'What is it, Nell?' asked her mum. 'You look worried.'

Did worry show that much? 'Nothing's the matter,' lied Nell.

A car drove into the yard and there were two heavy clunks in the porch: Mr Shepherd taking off his wellies. 'Where's Will?' he asked as he came into the kitchen. 'I've got something to show him.'

'He's in his . . . no he's . . .' Nell didn't know what to say. Her face was burning.

She tried again. 'I think he's . . . he's busy.'

'It doesn't matter,' said her dad. 'I'll show it to him later.'

But it did matter. The sky was so dark now, and the wind was growing stronger.

While her mum and dad were having a cup of tea, Nell crept out to the hall and quietly slipped on her wellies. Carefully, very carefully, she put on her anorak and pulled the hood over her head. Softly, very softly, she opened the back door, tiptoed out and closed it carefully behind her. Then she ran, ran, ran to the sycamore tree.

Will wasn't on the platform or the swinging rope ladder. Where was he?

'Will!' Nell called. 'Will, where are you?'

There was a moan quite close and then Nell saw Will. He was huddled on his side with a big plank lying on top of him.

'Will, what happened?' cried Nell.

'I slipped off the platform,' groaned Will, 'and the plank fell too. It hit my head, and my legs hurt when I move them.'

Nell noticed that he didn't even have his anorak on. She was about to point this out, but instead she said, 'Can I tell Mum and Dad where you are, now?'

'I think you'd better,' said Will.

★

The next day Will was ill. He had a terrible cold, a big bruise on his forehead and he'd sprained both his ankles. The birthday party was put off for a week.

Nell went to give her brother his present. It was a book that he'd always wanted, about spaceships. Will was sitting up in bed. His nose was red and he had a big bump on his forehead. 'Wow, thanks,' he said when he'd opened his present. And then, dropping his voice, he whispered, 'Nell, could you climb up to the tree-house for me, the almost-tree-house?'

'Me? Why?' Nell was astonished.

'I left my anorak there and Gran's present's in the pocket.'

'You really want me to climb up to your almost-tree-house?' Nell had to make sure.

'*Yes!*' Will said, rather loudly this time. 'I can't get there 'cos I'm ill. But you're well, aren't you?'

'I'm always well,' said Nell.

A few minutes later she was climbing up to the tree-house platform. When she got there she stood still for a moment, gazing down at the house and the fields and, far away, the dark roofs of the village. It was a beautiful day, the wind had dropped and the sunshine warmed her face.

Nell smiled to herself. 'I got here,' she said. 'I got to the almost-tree-house.'

2. Will's new bicycle

One of Will's birthday presents was a new bicycle. He wasn't allowed outside on his birthday, so Mr Shepherd wheeled it into the yard beneath Will's window and shouted, 'Look, Will! A present to make up for the tree-house.'

Will's head ached and his throat was so sore it seemed as though he had swallowed broken glass. But the sight of the shiny red bike cheered him up. He waved at his dad and stuck his thumbs in the air. 'Thanks, Dad!' he croaked.

The next minute Nell was there, smiling

up at him and patting the bike's smart red saddle.

Mr Shepherd asked her to take it back into the garage but, as soon as she took the handle-bars, Will began  thumping on the window-pane. 'It's not yours,' he wheezed. 'Leave it alone.'

'I'm not going to ride it!' she shouted as she wheeled the bike away. She wished her brother wouldn't get so angry about things. 'One day he'll explode,' she muttered.

It was Saturday, and Nell was expecting her friend, Fiona, to come over in the afternoon. She always brought her wellies when she came to see Nell. 'That farm's such a mucky place,' her mother complained. Mrs Strange was rather nervous about Fiona's visits to the Shepherds' farm. There were so many dangers: angry bulls, vicious cockerels, slippery paths, muddy dogs and duck ponds.

'Fiona mustn't do anything dangerous,' Mrs Strange told Mrs Shepherd.

'Of course not,' said Mrs Shepherd. 'I'm sure Fiona will be sensible.'

'Sometimes Nell leads her on, you know,' said Mrs Strange.

This wasn't true, but Nell and Mrs Shepherd didn't say anything. They were too polite to point out that it was the other way round.

When Mrs Strange had

gone, Nell and Fiona put on their wellies and went outside.

'What's that?' said Fiona when she saw the almost-tree-house.

Nell told her it was Will's tree-house. 'But it's not finished, yet,' she said.

'I'm going to climb that rope ladder,' said Fiona.

'Better not,' Nell advised. 'You might fall.'

'Nah,' said Fiona. She ran to the ladder and began to climb. One, two, three. She was three rungs up. The ropes swung about like snakes.

'Slower,' warned Nell. 'The rope ladder's very slippery.'

'Nah!' said Fiona. She lifted her foot for

the next step, but the heel of her wellie caught in the rope. For a moment Fiona wobbled and screamed, and then, THUMP, she was on the ground. Her jeans were all muddy and her knees were cut and bruised.

Nell took her indoors to get patched up, and that's where they stayed for the rest of the day. 'I think you'll be safer playing inside,' said Mrs Shepherd.

Mr Shepherd took Fiona home after tea. Before he got back there was a phone call for Mrs Shepherd. It was Fiona's mum.

'I don't want Fiona to come to the farm for a while,' Mrs Strange told Nell's mum. 'It's too risky. She's always having accidents.

Her knees are in a terrible state.'

'Nell's never had an accident,' said Mrs Shepherd.

'Nell can come to our house if she wants,' said Mrs Strange. 'I know she's Fiona's best friend.'

Nell didn't want to go to Fiona's house. Fiona had three little brothers who made a racket and followed them everywhere.

'I suppose I'll just have to stay at home with Will,' she said. Her dreams of a tea party in the tree-house were beginning to fade.

When he was better, the first thing Will wanted to do was to ride his new bike.

'Go carefully,' warned Mr Shepherd. 'It's much bigger than your old bike.'

'I'm always careful,' said Will.

His mum and dad and sister rolled their eyes.

'I'll just ride it down the lane to start with,' he said.

Nell went with him. She rode her pale blue bicycle with butterflies painted on the saddle, and she put on her safety helmet, just in case.

'You don't need that,' said Will. 'We're not going on the main road.'

'All the same,' said Nell. 'Accidents can happen.'

Jessie the sheepdog ran after the children, barking for joy. There was nothing she liked better than chasing bicycles. She was very unpopular with the postman.

After riding up and down the lane four times, Will wanted to try something different. 'I think I'll take the bike up the sheep-track to the top of the hill, and then whizz down,' he said. 'After all, it is a mountain bike.'

Nell thought the hill was rather steep, even for a mountain bike. She followed Will up to the fields and then watched him wheel his bike to the top of the hill. Jessie sat beside Nell with her ears pricked forward and her tail thumping, just as if she were expecting some excitement.

Nell hooked her finger in Jessie's collar. 'You can't chase Will this time,' she said. 'You'll cause an accident.'

Jessie looked up at Nell and whined.

'You can't race him either,' said Nell.

Will was slowing down now. The hill became very steep for the last few metres, too steep, Nell thought, for a bicycle. She wished Will would stop where he was and ride down. But on he went, pushing and puffing.

When Will was almost at the top of the hill, Nell saw the bullocks. They were coming round the side of the hill, six of them. They weren't as big as Mr Shepherd's prize bull, but they were lively and rough. Time and again, Mr Shepherd had told his children not to go into the bullocks' field. 'They're heavy animals,' he said, 'and very inquisitive. They don't mean to hurt, but when they're running they could knock you over in a second.'

'Look out, Will!' Nell called. 'Don't ride down, the bullocks are coming.'

Will took no notice. Perhaps he couldn't hear her. He turned his bike and swung his leg over the saddle.

'No, Will!' screeched Nell.

'Wheeeee!' cried Will as he came sailing down the track.

Jessie leaped up and down barking furiously. All at once she broke away from Nell and ran towards Will.

'Get out of the way!' Will yelled at the dog.

'Jess, come back!' cried Nell.

Will tried to slow down. Jessie was running up the track right in front of him. 'Jess!' he shrieked. He braked suddenly. The bike stopped, but Will didn't.

He flew over the handlebars and landed on his head.

Nell did some very quick thinking. I've got my helmet on, so I won't get hurt as badly as Will. She ran up to him, keeping an eye on the bullocks. They were very interested in Will's accident. In fact, they were pounding closer and closer.

'You've got to get up, Will!' Nell shouted. 'The bullocks are coming.'

Jessie ran at the bullocks, yelping and growling, but they took no notice. She was a sheep-dog, not a bull-dog. Her barking only made the bullocks more excited.

Nell reached her brother and pulled him to his feet. 'Now run,' she said. 'As fast as you can.'

'My bike,' moaned Will. 'I can't leave my bike.'

'I'll bring the bike,' said Nell. 'I've got a helmet on. You just run.'

Will limped as fast as he could towards the gate, while Nell pulled the bike upright and began to wheel it down after Will. Will's new bike was much heavier than hers, the handle-bars were high and awkward to hold and she found she couldn't run. She kept tripping up. The bullocks were snorting now, in a very unfriendly way. She could almost feel their breaths on her neck. She'd never make it to the gate if she didn't run faster.

Will had reached the gate and, as he swung himself on to the bars, he saw Nell and the bike. The bullocks were just a few metres behind her.

27

'Leave the bike, Nell!' he shouted. 'Or you'll be trampled!'

Nell didn't need telling a second time. She dropped the bike and ran. Behind her she heard a horrible scrunching noise as the bullocks ran over the bike. It seemed to hold them up a bit; just long enough for Nell, racing like the wind, to reach safety.

Will and Nell tumbled over the gate and dropped into the mud, just in time. The bullocks snorted at them, banging their heads on the bars and stamping in the muddy pools behind the gate.

Jessie didn't bother with the gate, she came flying over the wall, yelping in panic.

'It's your fault!' cried Will. 'You silly sheepdog. Look at my bike.'

The bullocks were playing with Will's brand new bike. It was a sorry sight. The spokes were broken, the saddle had come off and the handlebars were bent. It hardly

looked like a bike at all.

When Will and Nell staggered into the kitchen, Will was trying hard not to cry. His hair was full of mud and he had another bruise on his head.

'Whatever's happened?' cried Mrs Shepherd.

Out came the sad tale of the bullocks and the bike.

'My head aches,' moaned Will.

'What about you, Nell?' asked Mrs Shepherd. 'Were you hurt?'

'Not at all,' said Nell. 'I had my safety helmet on. I'm quite well.'

3. Two angry rams

Will felt much better in the morning. 'D'you think you could finish the tree-house today?' he asked his father.

'I haven't got time to build a tree-house,' said Mr Shepherd. 'There's too much to do.' He was trying to mend Will's bike. An impossible task.

'How about the day after that?' asked Will. 'I mean, it was supposed to be my birthday present.'

'I bought you a bike instead,' his dad reminded him.

'But my bike's all smashed up,' grumbled Will.

'And whose fault's that?'

Jessie gave a loud bark, almost as if she were owning up.

'It was Jessie's fault,' said Will, glaring at the sheepdog. Jessie wagged her tail.

'No use blaming it on a dog,' said Mr Shepherd.

Will's new friend, Martin Doyle, had promised to bring his bike round on Saturday. They were going to ride all round the farm, maybe even do some tricks on the stone walls. Now Will hadn't got a bike to ride.

'You can borrow mine,' Nell offered.

'It's a girl's bike,' sniffed Will

Nell ignored this. 'What about your old bike?'

'It's not a mountain bike and both the tyres are flat,' Will said.

Nell didn't bother to suggest Will mend his tyres, even though she knew he'd done it before. She decided that her brother just wanted to be miserable. Perhaps his head still ached.

'You're lucky to have a friend,' Nell muttered. 'Fiona's mum won't let her come here any more.'

Will suddenly felt sorry for his sister. 'You can come round with Martin and me,' he said. 'As long as you just watch when we're doing dangerous stuff.'

Nell brightened up. She wondered what sort of dangerous stuff they might do. 'I'll just watch,' she promised.

On Saturday morning, Jessie's barking woke Nell up. Jessie only barked like that when strangers came into the yard. Nell got out of bed and ran to the window.

Standing just inside the gate was a boy with curly hair. He was holding tight to the handlebars of a shiny black bike. Jessie was running round him, snapping excitedly.

Nell opened the window. 'Stop that, Jessie!' she shouted. 'Leave him alone!'

Jessie whined and sat down.

The boy grinned up at Nell. 'Thanks,' he said. 'I'm Martin Doyle. I've come to see Will.'

Nell put on her slippers and ran down to open the door, but Will had already brought his friend into the kitchen. He'd had his breakfast and was keen to show Martin the farm.

'Please be careful, Will,' said Mrs Shepherd. 'Don't do anything silly. Martin isn't used to farms.'

'We'll be careful,' said Will.

What was all that talk about dangerous stuff? Nell ran upstairs to get dressed. After breakfast she decided to go and find the boys. She hoped Will hadn't changed his mind about her going round with them.

She found Will and Martin in the almost-tree-house. Mr Shepherd had managed to do a bit more work on it and now it had one whole wall of planks, as well as a floor. Martin was very impressed. 'You can see for miles,' he said. 'D'you want to come up, Nell?'

'There's no room,' Will said quickly. 'And she'd hurt herself climbing the rope ladder.'

'I've done it before,' Nell called up to him, 'when you wanted me to fetch your birthday present.'

Will took no notice. 'Let's go down and see the pigs,' he said.

For the rest of the morning, Nell followed Will and Martin round the farm. They looked at the tractors in the barn, climbed trees in the wood and took it in turns to ride Martin's bike down the lane. Will ignored Nell but at least he didn't tell her to go away. Now and again Martin looked back and gave her a smile, so it wasn't too bad. It would have been a lot better if she'd had her own friend to talk to, though.

After a while, Nell decided she didn't want to follow the boys any more. She went and sat on the swing, where she had a good view of the almost-tree-house. She imagined how it would look with a roof and a window, maybe even a chimneypot, just for show.

Mr Shepherd walked past, looking rather the worse for wear. 'I've had a bad time with those rams,' he told Nell. 'They're always so angry when I take them away from their wives.' He laughed and Nell felt

better. Every winter Mr Shepherd had to separate the rams and the ewes. The ewes would have their lambs soon after Christmas and the rams were very jealous.

The Shepherds had two rams; Nell called them Ralph and Rupert. Will couldn't tell them apart, but Nell would always know Ralph, she'd fed him with a bottle when he was just a lamb. He was bigger and stronger than Rupert and his horns were longer.

Nell thought she would take Ralph and Rupert a treat to cheer them up. They were very fond of little apples. There was a store of apples in the barn, and Nell went to choose two of the smallest.

Will and Martin had completely vanished and Nell felt slightly anxious about Martin. She hoped Will wasn't leading him into danger.

The sun was going down and a fine mist was beginning to creep over the hills. Soon it would be dark. Nell hurried up to the field where Ralph and Rupert spent the winter. She could hear a gate banging and she had an uncomfortable feeling that something was not quite right.

Nell could see the field now. Ralph and Rupert were standing together by the wall. The two boys were sitting on top of the gate and Will was banging the bars with his feet.

'Don't tease them!' Nell shouted. 'They're very angry today!'

As usual, Will paid no attention to her. In fact, quite distinctly, she heard him say, 'Come on!' and, to Nell's horror, Will jumped into the field. Martin slid down after him.

Ralph and Rupert looked at the two boys and Nell could almost see the rams making up their minds: you go for Will and I'll get Martin.

Will began to run round the side of the field. Ralph lowered his head and charged. Rupert was just about to run at Martin when Nell reached the gate. She threw the apples into the field and Rupert hesitated, just long enough for Martin to hurl himself over the gate to safety.

'Phew!' he gasped. 'Will said those rams were friendly.'

'Not today,' said Nell.

Ralph was pounding after Will and

when Will tried to climb the wall, Ralph's horns caught up with his bottom. What happened next was quite spectacular. Will flew. With a bloodcurdling yell he soared into the air, his arms spread out like long skinny wings.

'Wow!' breathed Martin. 'That must have hurt.'

Will dropped on to the grass with a

moan. Luckily he was on the right side of the wall.

Nell and Martin helped Will back to the house. Will couldn't speak, he just kept moaning. When he got home he stumbled upstairs and lay on his bed, face down. Mrs Shepherd rang the doctor.

Martin's mother came to fetch him after tea and Mrs Shepherd explained what had happened. 'I'm afraid Will's always in the wars,' she said.

'What about Nell?' asked Mrs Doyle. 'Are you always in the wars, too?'

'No,' said Nell. 'I'm always well.'

'Ill Will and Well Nell,' laughed Martin.

Nell thought that Mrs Doyle would be cross about the rams. After all, Martin had

been in danger, but she only said, 'Boys will be boys.'

'You saved me, Nell,' said Martin as he left. 'See you!'

When the Doyles had gone, Nell went to look at the almost-tree-house. Will would never know if she climbed into it now. He would be lying down for quite a while. Before she could change her mind, she scrambled up the ladder and sat on the platform. A big white moon was rolling up behind the hills and all the trees looked soft and silvery.

'What have you been up to?' asked Mrs Shepherd when Nell came in.

'Just thinking,' Nell said.

4. Chickenpox

Will was a striker in the school football team. He was just about the best player, as he scored all the goals. There was to be a very important match in two weeks' time but, with two big bruises on his bottom, Will found it hard to run. Without him the school might lose the match.

Each day Will found he could walk a little faster. After a week he could run. But could he run fast enough? And could he score a goal? Nell helped out. After

school she would play football with Will in the field behind the house. The one without the rams.

After another week, Mr Simms, the P.E. teacher, said Will was well enough to play in the match.

'Just in time,' Will told Nell. It was Thursday and the match was on Saturday.

That night Will said he had a bit of a headache.

'Nerves,' said Mr Shepherd. 'You'll be fine tomorrow.'

Will wasn't fine. In the middle of the night he was sick. Next morning when he came down to breakfast he had two spots on his forehead. Even as Nell watched, more began to appear.

'One of the boys in our class has got chickenpox,' said Nell. 'It looked just like that.'

'Oh dear!' Mrs Shepherd stared at Will. 'I think you've got it, Will.'

Will did have chicken-pox. He had to miss the football match and the school team lost. To cheer him up, Mr Shepherd promised to finish the tree-house. He worked on it all weekend.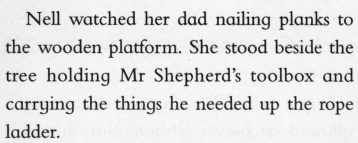

Nell watched her dad nailing planks to the wooden platform. She stood beside the tree holding Mr Shepherd's toolbox and carrying the things he needed up the rope ladder.

The tree-house grew and grew. Soon there were four walls and a big space for a window. Next came the roof. This seemed to be the hardest part. Mr Shepherd's hammering rang out across the hills. It was a wonderful roof with beams and roofing-felt. Mrs Shepherd provided a small table, two chairs and a piece of carpet. The tree-house would be warm and dry inside.

In a few days Will felt better, but he wasn't allowed to go to school. Not that this worried him. He spent all his time in the tree-house. He pulled things up in a bucket attached to a pulley: soldiers, Lego, books, pencils, cars, marbles, and even a giant model of Darth Vader. Tiger, the cat, climbed up by himself. He'd decided to live there for a while.

'Have you got cups and saucers?' Nell asked.

'Why would I want them?' said Will. 'I can drink out of a bottle.'

Obviously he didn't plan to have a tea party.

Still, Nell had something to look forward to. Soon there was to be a school trip to Blainey castle. Her teacher, Mrs Tinker, had told them all about it. Nell loved castles. She loved the narrow, curving stairs, the huge stone towers and the deep, dark dungeons. She could almost see the archers on the battlements with their bows and arrows. She could imagine knights on white chargers thundering across the drawbridge, and medieval ladies in long, floaty dresses. Did

they use cups and saucers? Nell wondered. Or plates with flowers on them?

Mrs Tinker didn't want Will to come back to school until he was quite free of chickenpox. She was expecting a baby and she didn't want to catch anything nasty before the baby arrived. So, although Will didn't feel ill, he couldn't go to school. Two days before the school trip, the doctor said Will wasn't infectious any more.

'Just in time!' Will cried. 'I can go to Blainey castle, after all.'

Nell thought it was rather unfair that Will had been let off school for so long, and then got to go on the school trip. She wondered if

Will would fall in the moat, or tumble down one of the curving staircases. I'd better keep an eye on him, she thought, he's missed too much school already.

Next morning Nell woke up with a headache. It was just a little headache, not bad enough to make her miss the school trip. She got dressed and started to brush her hair. When she looked in her mirror she noticed a blob on her chin, there were two more on her forehead and another one on the bridge of her nose. Could they be spots?

'No,' whispered Nell. She had an idea. If she pulled her hair over her face no one would see the spots. She nearly fell down the stairs on her way to breakfast. She could hardly see a thing because she'd brushed her hair over her face instead of behind her ears.

'Nell, whatever have you done with your hair?' asked Mr Shepherd.

'It's the latest style,' said Nell. She tried to get a spoonful of Cornflakes through to her mouth, but missed and spilled them all over the table – and her hair.

'You can't see what you're doing.' Mrs Shepherd pulled Nell's hair away from her face. 'Oh, my goodness, you've got chickenpox!' she said.

'No,' wailed Nell.

'I'm afraid you have,' said her mum. 'You can't

possibly go to school today.'

'But I feel well!' cried Nell.

'You might get worse,' Mrs Shepherd told her. 'It's no good, Nell. If you go to school, Mrs Tinker will just send you home.'

Nell burst into tears. 'I want to go to Blainey castle,' she sobbed. 'I've been thinking about it for days and days.'

'I'm sorry, Nell,' said her mum.

'It's not fair,' cried Nell. 'It's all Will's fault. He gave me the chickenpox.'

She noticed that Will was staring at her in a very odd way. He looked really upset about something. 'You can go in my tree-house,' he said. 'In fact, you can go there anytime you want, any, any time. I promise.'

'I don't want to go in the tree-house,' moaned Nell. 'I want to go to Blainey castle.'

It was no good. Nell's parents wouldn't let her go on the school trip. When Will left with his anorak and sandwiches, she muttered, 'I hope it rains,' and then changed her mind and called out, 'Have a good time!'

'I mean it about the tree-house!' Will called back.

Nell sat in the kitchen feeling very sorry for herself. 'I don't feel ill,' she told her mum. 'I'm never ill. I'm always well.'

The telephone rang and Mrs Shepherd picked up the receiver. 'Oh, I'm so sorry,' she said. 'What a shame. No, I'm afraid

Will's gone back to school. Never mind. Another time.' She put down the receiver and then frowned, the way she did when an idea was coming.

'That was Mrs Doyle,' she told Nell. 'Martin's got chickenpox, too, and he can't go on the school trip. Mrs Doyle wanted him to come and spend the day with Will. I was wondering . . . would you like Martin to come here?'

'If he wants,' said Nell. 'But he won't. He's Will's friend.'

'We'll see,' said her mum, and she rang Mrs Doyle.

Martin was very keen to spend the day at the farm. He didn't mind at all that Nell was at home and not Will. In fact he had a brilliant idea.

'Let's pretend we're at Blainey castle, hundreds of years ago,' he said.

'And you can be a knight!' cried Nell,

instantly cheering up. 'And I'll be a lady in a long floaty dress.'

'And the tree-house will be your tower,' said Martin.

'And Jessie can be your horse,' said Nell.

Later that morning, Nell and Martin climbed up to the tree-house.

Nell wore one of her mum's long dresses and a shawl for a cloak. Martin wore Will's grey balaclava and a long red towel. He left his horse beside the tree, with a bone to keep her quiet. When Nell pointed out that horses

didn't eat bones, Martin said, 'It's not a
bone, it's a parsnip.' He had a wonderful
imagination.

Mrs Shepherd put a pot of tea in Will's pulley-bucket, with two cups and saucers, two flowery plates and a bag of ham sandwiches. Very carefully Nell pulled it up through the window. She set out the plates and cups on the table and began to pour the tea. But when Martin's cup was half full, she suddenly stopped pouring.

'You don't mind drinking out of a cup, do you?' she asked, thinking of Will.

'Not at all,' said Martin.

'Or eating off flowery plates?'

'Not a bit,' said Martin.

Everything Nell ate seemed to taste delicious, even the custard tarts that Martin had brought.

It began to rain and the gentle drumming of raindrops on the tree-house roof made it seem, somehow, all the more cosy.

'I reckon this is better than Blainey castle,' said Martin, happily licking his fingers.

Nell had to agree. Tea in the tree-house was even more wonderful than she had imagined.